Sorcerers Always Lie

AMY LAURENS

OTHER WORKS

Find other works by the author at www.amylaurens.com

Sorcerers Always Lie

INKLET #78

AMY LAURENS

Inkprint PRESS

www.inkprintpress.com

Copyright © 2022 Amy Laurens

All rights reserved. No part of this book may be reproduced in any form or by any electronic or mechanical means, including information storage and retrieval systems, without permission in writing from the publisher, except by a reviewer, who may quote brief passages in a review.

This is a work of fiction. All characters, organisations and events are the author's creation, or are used fictitiously.

Print ISBN: 978-1-922434-18-0
eBook ISBN: 9798201821791

www.inkprintpress.com

National Library of Australia Cataloguing-in-Publication Data
Laurens, Amy 1985 –
Sorcerers Always Lie
50 p.
ISBN: 978-1-922434-18-0
Inkprint Press, Canberra, Australia
1. Young Adult Fiction—Fantasy—Dark Fantasy 2.
Young Adult Fiction—Fantasy—Romance 3. Young
Adult Fiction—Short Stories, Collections & Anthologies

First Print Edition: March 2022
Cover photo © Enrique Meseguer via Pixabay
Cover design © Inkprint Press
Interior art © Amy Laurens

SORCERERS ALWAYS LIE

THE FIRST PROBLEM WAS THAT ADELA'S left hand was still on fire. Not literally, of course, though it might as well have been: the tiny, red-gold sparks of glowing light embedded through it were the remains of a magical bullet, a bullet that had exploded into a softball-sized sphere of pain and light, like a very localised, very painful firework.

The cold making Adela's teeth chatter didn't help, goosebumps prickling her bare arms as she tried to make her mind focus on the dark, snow-crusted forest around her.

The dark trees—spruces, maybe, or some kind of pine, Adela had never been good at botany, although she'd learned to identify food and medical plants per force over the last few months—definitely they were some kind of conifers, though, broad with branches almost sweeping the ground, and they skulked, seeming to move and dance in the corners of her eyes.

The whole moonlit scene kept sliding in and out of focus, as though clouds were passing over the face of the full moon, even though the sky was cloudless and the stars twinkled fiercely.

She inhaled deeply, trying to force herself to calm through the pain.

They definitely smelled coniferous, with that cold, green, sappy smell.

Could have been her imagination, though, as her stomach roiled in response to the constant burn of her hand.

Focus, Adela. Don't worry about dancing trees, or flicking moonlight, or the fire alight in your hand. Focus.

There was grass under her feet, thick and green like a cultivated lawn.

Surely it was too cold here for that kind of grass?

Adela stared at it dazedly, sure she was missing something.

Usually, her brain moved at the speed of light, drawing connections between things faster than most people could blink. Usually, it would have taken her a matter of minutes to weave the spells to form a protective bubble around the campsite, shielding the tent from passersby—not that any passersby seemed terribly likely here, wherever here was.

But Adela and her two friends—and Jiri, mustn't forget Jiri, saving him was the whole reason they were in this mess to begin with—had broken camp in a hurry and vanished through to God only knew where—none of them had recognised it when they'd arrived, although *one* of them had to have, for the group to have transported here in the first place—and her hand was still on fire.

It seared, in much the same way as your hand might if you were ever dumb enough to stick it into a camp fire and hold it there, Adela imagined —not that she'd ever had any personal experience in being so stupid.

The boys, though? Well. They were both House Liione. It was practically a right of passage at the Sibelius Sorcery Academy to do dumb crap in the name of bravery and courage.

I mean, Adela clarified to herself, because concentrating on this inner monologue was helping her to rationalise the pain, helping her to avoid panic, because the body's natural response to this much pain was sheer and bloody panic, and Adela couldn't say she blamed her body very much…

She inhaled sharply again, filling her nose with the sharp scent of snow-laden air. That line of thinking was unproductive.

No, she told herself. *To finish my earlier thought, Bug isn't so bad when it comes to stupid dares.* At least he was the one who'd had the sense to put a stop to the Liione boys competing to see who could balance the longest on top of their dorm's upper balustrade—the one with the three-storey drop on one side of it.

Leroy, he was the one you had to watch out for, always doing dumb stuff to prove he was as good as his brothers, or his friends, or whatever larger spectre was haunting him that particular day.

Adela winced. That made her sound unnecessarily cruel. Actually, she liked

Leroy—she liked him quite a lot, maybe even like-liked him—at least, that was what she'd been telling herself for the last month, ever since bloody *Jiri* had rescued her from the hellhole of his uncle's house, releasing her from daily torture, both mental and physical, as her captors tried to ply the whereabouts of Bug from her.

She hadn't given in then, and she wouldn't give in to this pain now. It wasn't the first time she'd copped a magic bullet during this stupid, infernal war, and it wouldn't be the last.

But of course, there was the crux of the second problem: although she could block the panic from rising so long as she kept up a clear and dispassionate internal dialogue, the moment she stopped that and tried to focus on actually doing some magic, the whole, fragile thing fell apart, and the panic came roaring back as a flood of adrenalin in the pit of her stomach, a vice around her chest, the threat of hyper-ventilation.

She couldn't do magic while she was panicking. She couldn't not panic while she was trying to do magic. And if she couldn't do magic, couldn't get their bubble shield raised asap, they'd be almost literal sitting ducks, stuck out here God only knew where in the middle of some freezing wilderness, waiting for the enemy to find them.

Adela shivered violently, both from the effort of fighting off the panic and from the sudden gust of wind that washed over her, cutting through her too-thin long-sleeved shirt. It had been cool back in the other forest, the one where her hand had been hit, where Jiri—

She stamped on that line of thought.

It was much colder here, now, wherever here and now was—did *any-one* know where they'd vanished to?—

and that was all that mattered.

Because if she didn't get the bubble up quickly, it wouldn't matter how long it took the enemy to find them—they'd probably die of exposure overnight first.

Adela glanced up at the stars, dancing in and out of the patchy cloud cover, and tried to work out what the time might be. It had been around midnight when she'd woken in the other forest from that drea—uh, because she couldn't sleep.

She'd gotten up, gotten dressed, wandered out to the edge of the bubble... And Jiri had happened, and so had the shot to her hand. Less than an hour. Add in some time for the boys to hurriedly pack their tents after they'd been discovered, and then they'd vanished, and so it was probably a little after one.

Which meant that there were still colder hours to come.

Adela shivered again, a full-bodied shake that rattled her from her teeth to her toes.

Jiri. Urgh. If he hadn't suddenly turned up outside their bubble, if she hadn't felt morally obligated to leave her protection and rescue him when people had started shooting at him, she wouldn't have been injured, they wouldn't have been discovered, they wouldn't have had to break camp in the middle of the night—and she wouldn't be stuck out here, alone in the sporadic starlight, hugging herself tightly to stop the shivers in air that smelled of snow and conifers, trying to fight down the fire in her hand so she could stop panicking and make magic.

A hand on her shoulder sent her jumping a foot into the air as she whirled around, good hand splayed and at the ready for some kind of magical protective spell, even if her mind wasn't stilled and prepared.

"Whoa, Della, it's me," said Leroy soothingly, both hands up where she could see them. "Sorry. I did scuff my feet," he added.

Adela inhaled quickly and deeply through her nose, sucking in air like she'd been drowning, and gave him a curt nod. Even in the moonlight, his red hair gleamed, and if her hand hadn't felt like it was about to take off for higher planes, she might have been brave enough to run her fingers through it.

Adela bit the inside of her lip, but concentrating on Leroy's hair did seem to be another productive way to ignore the pain. And it wasn't like he seemed to mind or anything.

Actually, he was staring at her, brows knit, mouth slightly down-turned. "Adela? Della? You okay?"

He said it like maybe he'd said it once or twice already, and maybe he had. Another shiver rattled through

Adela's body, her teeth chattering violently.

Bloody hand. If only it would stop flaming she could get the shields up and protect them, warm the air up a little.

Leroy had said something again, and she'd missed it. She shook her head.

Ope, don't do that, she told herself as dizziness washed over her.

She shivered again—and then Leroy was there, holding her tight, rubbing her back and her biceps bracingly, murmuring in her ear.

Adela blinked heavily—tired, so tired—and let herself sag against Leroy for a moment, her face pressed into his chest.

Probably, there were more sounds —was that Bug, joining them? He was talking to her—no, to Leroy—to her? Leroy? Both of them? She couldn't follow it—and it was cold, and her hand was on fire, and she couldn't make out what either of them were saying over the sound of her pulse in her ears, the feel of her heartbeat in her burning hand, the metallic hint of blood in the back of her throat.

It was dark, and she was lying down. Adela's hand still hurt, but it was a slow, lingering burn, not a fierce blaze—like maybe she'd stuck her hand in a fire a week or so ago, rather than sometime in the last few minutes.

She snorted, moderately amused by her comparison, and realised her eyes were closed.

The tent. She was in the sleeping tent, moonlight pattering softly down on the walls, making them glow silver. Her mouth tasted sour, like she hadn't cleaned her teeth in a week—she *had*, thank you very much, it was Bug who had a questionable relationship with oral hygiene—and the air smelled musty, even though it was still cool. If they could manage to avoid being harassed or shot at for the next forty-eight hours, she'd air the sleeping bags out.

If.

So far, in the last couple of months, they'd been harassed, shot at, hexed, poisoned and/or had to run for their lives at least every second day, so the chances of airing the sleeping bags out were low, but whatever. A girl could hope.

Otherwise, it wasn't as though she wasn't *used* to musty sleeping bag smells (and often worse, sharing the tent as she did with two teenage boys, urgh).

Adela shifted on her bed—the one in the middle, the warmest spot, thanks chivalry—and adrenalin crashed through her system as she realised someone was in the tent with her, not in one of the beds right next to her, but in a new bed, a fourth one, over from the one on her right.

Heart hammering at her sternum, she lay completely still, trying to figure out how to look without being seen to look.

Slowly, gradually, she let her head slump to one side, as though perhaps she was falling asleep again. With her head on this angle, and her eyes slitted open, she saw the watcher: a shock of blond hair, gleaming bluish in the night light; a shadowy face, long, with a neat, pointed chin and strong jaw.

A second wave of adrenalin crashed over her at the realisation that she was sharing a tent with Jiri Talhallen, lying on his back at the very edge of the tent. She couldn't quite tell in this light if he was staring at her or not, but she closed her eyes furiously just in case.

In fact, who cared if he knew she was awake. She sniffed and rolled over, turning her back to him.

"Adela?" he said, and his voice was soft, weak, uncertain.

Damn him.

He'd probably never been shot before in his life, and while she'd only copped a bullet in the hand, he'd been hit right in the shoulder. The pain she'd been experiencing the last hour was stomach-retchingly bad, but she'd been hit in the shoulder once too, in the early days, right below her collarbone, and that kind of pain stayed with you till you died.

Sighing heavily, Adela rolled back over, curling up with her hands tucked underneath her cheek—her injured hand still hurt, but she'd obviously been asleep for a while and the slow burn she could feel now, well, she'd learned to ignore pain like this so, so well these last few months—and her knees pulled up to her chest, the un-zipped bag lying loosely over her.

"Am... am I dying?"

Adela snorted. "No," she said firmly. "No such luck."

Jiri inhaled shakily. "That's..." He winced, face crumpling distinctly even in the shadowy half-light. "Harsh," he said, but there was an edge of amusement to his voice, even though he could barely speak a sentence straight through the pain.

"I told you," Adela said without really thinking. "This is not happening. This is not a Thing."

Jiri sucked in a breath. "Sure... feels like a thing." He shifted awkwardly, babying his right shoulder, wincing again.

(Was it getting lighter in here? Surely she hadn't been able to see his face that well a second ago. How long had she slept? In the tent. With Jiri. Urgh!)

Adela rolled her eyes. "Not the bullet, you idiot. You know what I mean."

He did stare at her then, and it *was* growing lighter; she could see the intensity of his gaze. "Same side now, Adela. Remember?"

She scowled. "Only because of that stupid potion. It's not like you had a change of heart by yourself or anything."

His jaw twitched. "You're wrong," he said. "I didn't drink—" He stopped to inhale gaspily.

Adela rolled her eyes again at his wincing and reached out at full stretch to rest her good hand on his chest. "Lie still," she snapped. "It's not going to heal faster with you thrashing about like a beached baby seal." Experimentally, she pushed a trickle of magic through her body. Her injured left hand burned brighter as it drew energy in from the surroundings, but gritting her teeth, she felt a similarly-sized trickle exit her right hand and flow into Jiri.

He inhaled deeply in response, a clear breath with better chest movement than he'd managed yet.

Adela's brows knit together. It was only the tiniest of trickles; it shouldn't have worked *that* well to displace the pain.

But he was clearly feeling exponentially better, because he rolled over onto his left side to face her, injured shoulder in the air, hunching awkwardly.

Adela's good hand dropped to the spare bed in between them before she withdrew it and made her own deep inhalation, cheeks twitching as she clenched her jaw.

A subtle tang coloured the air, something rich and fruity and summery and intimately connected with the colour orange.

Immediately, Adela tried to stop breathing, because the last thing she needed was to be thinking about how good Jiri smelled, even after everything they'd been through in the last few hours.

"I didn't drink the potion so I'd know whether or not to rescue you," Jiri murmured.

Adela rolled onto her back and studied the pattern the leaves made in the slowly brightening light outside the walls of the tent. Goosebumps rose over her arms, and she pulled the sleeping bag up, warm and protective against the still-cold air. "Sure," she said, nonchalantly, like maybe she believed him.

That was the quintessential problem though, wasn't it. All sorcerers lied, all sorcerers except Adela, because all sorcerers—except Adela—could tell when anyone else was telling the truth.

It was stupid, but when everyone could tell when everyone else was telling the truth—and therefore infer when they weren't—magical Society had decided that the best way around this was to *never* tell the truth.

Every sorcerer was a liar.

Every sorcerer except Adela.

She swiped covertly at the one tear that had betrayed her by slipping down her temple—thankfully on the side away from Jiri—and reminded herself that killing him now would be a Very Bad Plan.

She could do it. She could probably do it. She'd loosed pretty bad hexes before, and although she hadn't stuck around to see the after effects, logic dictated that some of the people she'd attacked while this war raged had died.

It was easier to sleep at night by reminding herself that, statistically speaking, it was also *possible* they had survived.

But the fact remained that, if she really wanted to, she could probably kill Jiri where he lay. Especially since the shoulder wound would weaken his defences for a good week or so yet.

Of course, that meant her defences were similarly weakened, thanks to her stupid hand—which had only been injured because she'd risked her butt to save Jiri, of course. She scowled at the roof of the tent as though it had personally offended her.

"I promise," Jiri said softly, and abruptly Adela realised that he'd been staring at her this whole time. "I was going to rescue you anyway. If you thought about it for a second, you'd know that. You'd know."

It was probably true, and Adela hated it.

But you didn't just waltz into a prison cell carrying a quarter-million-dollar potion and offer to drink it with the prisoner on the off chance that it might tell you to release them.

And he had to have brewed the potion, the Anamata, recently; it had a forty-eight hour expiration date.

But still.

Tears slipped out of both eyes this time, and this time, Adela let them. "I can't tell if you're lying, Jiri," she said hoarsely. "You know I can't." And never, in her whole life, in six years of being tormented and judged and shunned for it, never had she hated her inability to sense lies more.

He reached out, not quite full stretch for him, but unable to reach further anyway because of his injured shoulder, and laid his hand softly on her cheek, gentle and warm in the cool predawn air, that same warm, orange, fruity smell lingering around him. "Adela," he whispered. "I can't promise never to lie."

She shook her head, one cutting jerk that dislodged his hand. "I don't—"

"Shh," he said, though he withdrew his hand back to safety. "I can't promise *never* to lie," he said again, voice rich and deep and raw, "but I promise you, I *promise*: I will never, ever lie to you when we are alone."

Adela shut her eyes, imagining a world where that was possible for just a fraction of a second. That sour taste still lingered in the back of her throat when she concentrated, and her hand still burned softly, intruding on even the possibility of such a world. "How can you possibly expect me to believe that?"

"Hey," he said softly, and she tilted her head toward his voice, opened her eyes to see him staring at her, blue eyes visible now in the early morning light, searching her gaze for the depths of her soul—and for just a moment, she let herself search back.

What's in there, Jiri? she wondered. *What are you really like, deep down in the depths of your self? What would you have been if you hadn't been born to a family of racist, classist pricks?*

Okay, that last one did it. Adela reached over and touched his cheek lightly with the fingertips of her injured left hand, a lingering brush against rough stubble before she withdrew to the security of her own space once again. "Jiri," she said softly. "This is never going to happen. I don't care what the Anamata said. You're not my future."

Even though, darn it, her pulse was fluttering like a butterfly right now, and her cheek glowed with the memory of his touch, and her fingers felt electric, as though his touch was enough to take away all the pain from the bullet, and she could imagine them skin to skin, close, so, so close, just like the start of one of her infernal dreams, and a tiny, curious part of her wondered—just wondered—if real life could ever be as good as a dream.

"Okay," Jiri said, ocean-dark eyes so sad Adela thought she might drown. He rolled onto his back and stared up at the brightening roof, and Adela fought with herself not to clutch after him.

They were dreams, she told herself sternly. *Nothing more. He is not a safe person.*

And I am not going to speak. I am not going to say something just so he'll turn and look at me. I am not an idiot. I like Leroy. Leroy is cute and has gorgeous, thick, red hair and lovely brown eyes, and he smells like pine and soap and he's kind, and he never killed anyone—well, at least until the stupid war started—and he never called me slurs or spread vicious lies about me or had racist, vicious family members.

Jordan excepting.

"I mean it," Jiri said, interrupting her internal monologue. "I know you won't believe me. But I mean it. I've never yet lied to you when we were alone, and I promise: I never will."

Adela snorted at that. "I thought sorcerers were supposed to be *good* at lying."

He cut her a sharp, questioning glance.

She shook her head in response, half irritated, half exasperated. "You told me, in your uncle's bedroom"— the place where she'd been imprisoned for several days, tortured to the edge of her sanity—"that you'd brought the Anamata so you'd know if you were supposed to set me free or not."

That was the beauty of Anamata, and the reason for its expense: a single dose would last you up to a year, deepening and clarifying your intuition and foresight, helping you to act in ways that furthered your most important goals.

It also, rumour had it, showed you the entirety of your future relationship with another person, if you drank it with them at the right time, in the right place, under the right circumstances.

Adela shook her head again and pressed her eyes closed. "You told me then you needed the potion to tell you if you should save me. You told me just now that you already *knew* you were going to save me." She tilted her head over to face him again, and gave him a small, sad smile that tasted of bitterness and felt like regret. "Which one was the lie, Jiri? And how will I believe you when you tell me?"

Jiri opened his mouth, closed it again, and pursed his lips, eyes soft and sad. He opened his mouth—

"Adela?" Leroy's call from in front of the tent dissipated the moment, and

Adela sat up, ready to greet Leroy, locking Jiri away into a deep, dark corner of her heart where the sadness couldn't get at her.

"I'm up," she said, pushing the bottle-green sleeping bag off her legs.

The tent zipped partly open, and Leroy's auburn mop of hair appeared toward the bottom of the tent door, his wide, freckled face appearing under it, eyebrows furrowed in concern. "How are you feeling?" he asked. "When you collapsed…"

Adela widened her eyes at him and cut a sharp glance at Jiri, ignoring the way that Jiri's eyebrows mirrored Leroy's. "I'm fine," she said firmly, and got to her feet to prove it, also ignoring the way the room of the tent spun a little as she did.

Leroy nodded. "Good," he said, and stood, unzipping the tent the rest of the way and offering Adela a hand. "Because I know you've been working with Bug on that silencing spell for weeks now, but he's still doing something wrong."

Adela bit the inside of her lip, but she couldn't stop her eyes from dancing. "But I'm sure *you* have the air compression layer of the bubble working perfectly," she said, voice as serious as she could manage.

Leroy snorted. "Of course I do." He took Adela by her good hand, and tucked her arm into his as she stepped out of the tent. "That's why we need you to come fix it all now, if you're up for it."

"Adela?"

Jiri's call was barely audible, but Adela glanced at him, her injured hand holding the tent zipper ready to close the door as she ignored the pain.

"I mean it," he said quietly, and the intensity of his gaze made Adela's breath catch. "Never when we're alone."

Her jaw twitched.

"What did he say?" Leroy asked.

Adela gave her head a brisk shake. "Nothing." She zhoozhed the tent closed hurriedly and settled herself on Leroy's arm, holding him just a little closer than she'd ever done before.

Leroy sniffed. "Bloody Jiri. Always causing trouble."

"Yeah," Adela agreed as they walked away from the tent, feet crunching in the thin, patchy snow on the ground. She glanced back once, the blue and silver dome of the tent glistening with dew, a light frosting of snow covering the evergreen conifers behind it, her breath silver and misty in front of her. The air smelled clean, and fresh, and for the first time in months, Adela had an intuition that maybe, just maybe, this would be a good few days to air the sleeping bags out after all.

THE MAKING OF *SORCERERS ALWAYS LIE*

This is the third of Adela's stories, and possibly the most fun to write so far. The dynamic between Adela and Jiri just writes itself, really. Case in point, this story—like the first two—was written in the car while I was waiting for my son to finish his gymnastics training.

Of course, where it's going from here is anybody's guess :'D

One day, I hope to sit down and finish a whole suite of these stories, because there's a key scene where they reunite as adults that I'm super looking forward to... But as for how they get there... Well, they do say it's the journey not the destination, right?

Read more by Amy Laurens!

ANAMATA

Adela huddled in the corner, praying nobody would remember she was there. The bedroom-turned-prison-cell was dark enough that she had trouble counting her fingers in front of her face, and the whole place stank of fear and misery, of human waste left to rot and fester, acrid urine burning her nose even as tears stung her eyes.

Her fingers were crammed into her mouth, something that usually would have been enough to make her puke with just the thought of what they might be covered in—but it was that, or let the sobs right out, and if she cried, someone would hear her, and if someone heard her, they'd take her out and torture her some more.

Probably they would anyway, and every tick and creak of the house cooling—it must be going night again; how many was that now? Three? Four? Something like that—might have been the sound of footsteps in the hall outside, coming to get her.

The first day hadn't been so bad. That was before they'd taken her and tried to break her—tried, because everyone always underestimated teenage girls, and they hadn't reckoned on her mental strength. She hadn't stayed alive for this long while war ravaged the countryside by being soft, or flighty.

And so: the first day had been bearable, even when she'd had to relieve herself in the corner, without even a bucket, because the room had been stripped of furniture except for the bare bones of the wooden slat bedframe and a single sheet—which, in her darker moments, Adela guessed was there purely so that someone desperate enough had a way to end it all, saving their captors the trouble.

The second day had been tolerable, because for a brief interval, she'd had company: an elderly, wizened man so stooped he was shorter than she was—which, given she could maybe hit five three in a decent pair of heels, was saying a lot.

He hadn't talked much, and he'd smelled of sour sweat and vomit, and the bright red scars over his back and shoulders and arms—torture wounds, sliced open and immediately healed by magic, but healed wrong, so they never stopped burning—had brought bile in the back of Adela's throat. That was what waited for her, eventually, when they ran out of other, slightly less painful ways to make her talk. Ripping out her fingernails, for example.

But regardless, he'd been someone else to talk to—talk *at*, anyway—and something to care for other than her own pitiful situation.

Because the truth of the matter was, the only way she was getting out of this was dead, or else if they broken her mind so hard she'd never be of use to anyone, in which case they *might* decide to be done with her and throw her out into the woods beyond the enchanted fence—but then she'd be dead within the day anyway, of exposure or thirst or caught in the crossfire of yet another skirmish.

A few months ago, the worst thing she could possibly imagine was failing her exams, because that would mean admitting that she wasn't a real sorcerer, that everyone else was right and genetics mattered after all, and the fact that she and she alone could use magic but not detect other people's lies like all the other sorcerers meant that she was somehow lesser, inferior, unimportant.

The day she'd arrived at the famous Sibelius Sorcery Academy, she'd vowed that no one would ever have an excuse to call her inferior again, not after that prat Jiri Tahallin with his white-blond hair and ocean-dark eyes had stood up in front of the whole school after the welcome dinner and denounced her as a dud while the scent of candle smoke and pumpkin pie spice mix filled the air, and the taste of despair and homesickness filled her throat.

Screw him. He hadn't known her then—and he hadn't learned any better in the interim, either, even though she'd been top of every class, always spreading rumours about how she must be cheating, must be getting help, or—in the last twelve months, about halfway through sixth year when he'd turned dark and broody—that maybe she was sleeping her way to the top.

Although, to be fair, it was his awful crony Hydrant—red of hair, ruddy of skin, prone to gushing—who'd come up with that one, and the black-haired idiot Gully who'd done most of the spreading, probably to try to get into Tahallin's good graces.

But right now, it was easier to be angry than to try to make excuses for him; no, not just easy, but possibly a matter of life and death, as Adela sat cross-legged, alone in the dark, trying to breathe shallowly against the urine stench, leaning her forehead against the cold, splintery leg of the bedframe, picking at the skin around her finger-nails because physical pain was con-crete, measurable, tangible, and it sure beat the vague, amorphous anxiety thrumming through her head.

The door opened.

Keep reading! Head to
www.inkprintpress.com/inklets/i47/
to buy your copy now!

ABOUT THE AUTHOR

AMY LAURENS is an Australian author of fantasy fiction for all ages.

As well as the *Changing Tides* stories, she has also written the award-winning portal-fantasy *Sanctuary* series about Edge, a 13-year-old girl forced to move to a small country town because of witness protection (the first book is *Where Shadows Rise*), the humorous fantasy *Kaditeos* series, following newly graduated Evil Overlord Mercury as she attempts to acquire a castle, the young adult series *Storm Foxes*, about love and magic and family in small town Australia, and a whole host of non-fiction and shorter works.

INKLETS

Collect them all! Released on the 1st and 15th of each month.

INKLET #079
Shadows
NEVER LIE
AMY LAURENS

INKLET #080
Here She Lies
LIANA BROOKS

INKLET #081
Perfect
Destruction
An Age Of Unicorns Story
AMY LAURENS

INKLET #082
What Blood
Can Do
AMY LAURENS

INKLET #083
Dancer, Dreamer
Seer
LIANA BROOKS

INKLET #084
As Time
Whirls Slowly
Past
AMY LAURENS

INKLET #085
Far More
Satisfying
Than Hell
AMY LAURENS

INKLET #086
Just
Another Day
In Hell
LIANA BROOKS

INKLET #087
Moon AND
Morning
AMY LAURENS

INKLET #088
Some
Impropriety
Expected
AMY LAURENS

INKLET #089
NEON SNOW
LIANA BROOKS

INKLET #090
Reincarnation
LIANA BROOKS

INKLET #091
More Than
Mushrooms
AMY LAURENS

DOUBLE ISSUE
INKLET #092
How To Make A Star
& The World Ended
LIANA BROOKS

INKLET #093
CAUGHT
IN THE ACT
AMY LAURENS

INKLET #094
ANUBIS
Has Sent You
Six Souls
LIANA BROOKS

INKLET #095
PRAYER TO A
GODDESS
LIANA BROOKS

INKLET #096
Love In The
Time Of Corona
AMY LAURENS